For Robert

Copyright © 1994 by Nick Sharratt

First U.S. edition 1994
Published in Great Britain in 1994
by Walker Books Ltd., London.

Library of Congress Cataloging-in-Publication Data
Sharratt, Nick.
My mom and dad make me laugh / Nick Sharratt.—1st U.S. ed.
Summary: Simon's mom likes spots and his dad likes stripes, but
Simon likes something different, and it isn't spotted or striped.
ISBN 1-56402-250-1
[1. Pattern perception—Fiction.] I. Title.
PZ7.S53234My   1994
[E]—dc20   93-3558

10 9 8 7 6 5 4 3 2 1

Printed in Italy

The pictures in this book were done in crayon.

Candlewick Press
2067 Massachusetts Avenue
Cambridge, Massachusetts 02140

My Mom and Dad Make Me Laugh

Nick Sharratt

CANDLEWICK PRESS
CAMBRIDGE, MASSACHUSETTS

My mom and dad make me laugh.

One likes spots, and the other likes stripes.

My mom likes spots in winter

and spots in summer.

My dad likes stripes on weekdays

and stripes on weekends.

Last weekend we went to the safari park. My mom put on her spottiest dress and earrings, and my dad put on his stripiest suit and tie.

I put on my gray shirt and pants.
"You sure like funny clothes!" said my mom and dad.

We set off in the car, and on the way we stopped for something to eat.
My mom had a spotty pizza, and my dad had some stripy ice cream.

I had a roll. "You sure like funny food!" said my mom and dad.

When we got to the safari park it was very exciting.

My mom liked the big cats best.

"Those are spectacular spots," she said. "And I should know!"

My dad liked the zebras best.

"Those are super stripes," he said. "And I should know!"

But the animals I liked best didn't have spots and didn't have stripes. They were big and gray and eating their lunch.

"Those are really great elephants," I said.

"And I should know!"